DET ZACK

and the Secret in the Storm

JERRY D. THOMAS

Pacific Press Publishing Association
Boise, Idaho
Oshawa, Ontario, Canada

Edited by Aileen Andres Sox
Designed by Dennis Ferree
Cover and inside art by Kim Justinen
Typeset in 13/16 New Century Schoolbook

ISBN 0-8163-1323-7

95 96 97 98 99 • 5 4 3 2 1

Dedication

To Michael, Caleb, and Zac
and their mom and dad,
who've already been through the storm
and already learned the secret.

Special congratulations to
Jacque Giem
of Sioux Falls, South Dakota,
the winner of the
Detective Zack Poster Contest
and thanks for
allowing Zack to use your name
in this adventure!

Other books by
Jerry D. Thomas

Detective Zack Danger at Dinosaur Camp
Detective Zack and the Missing Manger
　　Mystery
Detective Zack and the Mystery at Thunder
　　Mountain
Detective Zack and the Red Hat Mystery
Detective Zack and the Secrets in the Sand
Detective Zack and the Secret of Noah's Flood
Detective Zack's Word Puzzle Safari

Contents

Chapter | Page

1 Thunder in Texas 7

2 Chicken Wrestling 13

3 Strange Light in the Barn 23

4 A Mystery About God 31

5 Grown-ups and God 41

6 Clues in the Barn 51

7 Two Ideas, Two Suspects 61

8 Freedom and a Trap 71

9 Mistake in the Crate 79

10 The Mystery Is Solved—Wrong! 87

11 Hurricane Warning 97

12 Trapped Like Rabbits 105

13 Rescued From the Hurricane 115

14 Secret in the Storm 123

CHAPTER ONE

Thunder in Texas

Tropical Storm Jacque
Highest winds—42 miles per hour

Every time I pick up my pencil, lightning strikes. I don't mean it strikes me or my pencil, but it's close enough to make my writing wobble.

I'm trying to write in my notebook in the middle of a thunderstorm. Luckily, I'm not in the storm. I'm in the house—my grandparents' house. I guess they have a lot of thunderstorms down here in Texas.

Anyway, this thunderstorm is getting closer—and louder. Before I could even finish the last sentence—*flash! crash!*—lightning struck, and thunder shook the whole house. It isn't easy to write in the middle of a storm.

Still, it beats wrestling with chickens. I should know.

DETECTIVE ZACK

Grandpa's farm isn't really a farm. Mom says it used to be, but now it's just a big house surrounded by tall trees and open fields. Grandpa says it used to be farmland for miles around, but now there are lots of houses around and just a few old farms. Still, it's a great place to explore, especially when all our cousins are here too.

I just wish they had some animals. You know, a few horses or cows or sheep. Something normal like that. But no, all they keep are you-know-whats.

Chickens—a whole chicken pen full of chickens. And not just your normal everyday egg-laying chickens. These are prize-winning chickens that have been taking the blue ribbon at the county fair for years.

After the hello hugs to Grandma, Grandpa, and Uncle Trav, Kayla and I and our cousin, Dusty, headed straight out to the hay barn. Grandpa calls it the hay barn even though there are only a few bales of hay in it. The best thing about a hay barn is the hayloft, the big room upstairs where the bales of hay are stacked.

We claimed the loft as our fort when we were all here two summers ago. That time, we were busy escaping and hiding from little brothers, sisters, and cousins. The loft was the perfect place for that—the only way up was a wooden rung ladder nailed to one wall inside. And the little kids weren't allowed to climb it.

"I'll be the first one up," Dusty shouted as we raced through the barn door. He's a little younger than I, but older than Kayla.

"Good," Kayla called back. "You can check for spiders—and mice."

Dusty ran straight through to the big loading doors at the end of the loft and pulled out the board that held them closed. "Zack, help me push them open." With both of us pushing, the doors swung out, and our spying post was open for business.

"This is perfect," I said. "Even better than I remember."

"And dustier," Kayla added. She stared suspiciously in the corners.

Dusty sighed. "Too bad we don't have someone to spy on. This place looks deserted. There's nothing going on." He held up his binoculars. "The only things moving are clothes on the clothesline and chickens in the chicken pen."

"What about over there?" I asked. He focused on Millers' barn, another hay barn like Grandpa's, only much older looking. Grandpa says the old Miller house burned down about thirty years ago, and no one has lived on the property since then. Millers' barn stands just past Grandpa's property at the edge of the woods.

"It looks like no one's been near it since the last time we were here," Dusty reported.

From behind us, Kayla hissed. "Shh! Do you hear that?" she whispered.

At first, I thought she was talking about a spider or something. But before I could say anything, I heard it. Somewhere down below us in the barn, something or someone was making a rustling, scratching sound. Something that sounded big.

"What on earth is that?" I wondered. "Did Grandpa get a horse? Or a cow?"

Dusty shrugged. "I don't think so. Just chickens. But if that's a chicken, it must be the size of a cow!" We both put our ears to the floorboard to hear better.

"There it is again," I whispered. It made me nervous to hear something without being able to see it. It was a kind of scratching, scraping sound.

"Maybe it's just the wind," Kayla squeaked.

Suddenly, a head popped up through the hatch behind us. "Hey, what are you guys doing?" a voice asked.

Dusty and I turned so fast we almost cracked

heads. "What? Who?" Dusty stammered. "Oh, Sonia, it's you." He collapsed onto the floor.

"Didn't scare you, did I?" Sonia asked as she climbed out in the loft.

I had to frown. "That's what we heard. You stomping around down there."

Sonia and her family live on the next farm over past Millers' barn. You can just barely see the top of her house from the loft. Her dad, Mr. Tillman, is usually around, because Grandpa hires him to help do some of the heavy work around the farm. Sonia always comes over to play with Kayla when we're visiting.

Sonia nodded. "It wasn't me. I've been practicing being quiet. No one ever knows when I'm around. It was probably just a rat."

Kayla's eyes got big. "A rat? You don't think there are any up here, do you?" She started staring at the corners again. Sonia just laughed.

"You didn't hear anything strange?" Dusty asked. "Something that sounded big?"

Sonia shook her head. "You must have been imagining it. Sometimes, sounds in our barn sound louder than they really are. Once I thought someone was trying to knock one wall down when it was really just a woodpecker."

Before long, Grandma called us to supper. Sonia

headed for home, and we headed for the house. We walked right past the chicken pen. Well, I wish we had walked past it, but Kayla wanted to stop. I should have kept going.

"I think Grandma's got more chickens than ever," Dusty said as we walked up to the gate. From all over the fenced-in pen, white heads bobbed up, and the clucking sounds got louder.

Kayla stuck her head over the fence and stared. "Where's Old Red Top?" she asked. "Last time we were here, his crowing woke me up every morning."

I leaned over the gate next to her, but I couldn't see the old rooster either. As usual, the chickens came clucking over, looking for someone to feed them.

Bock, bock-bock. They crowded around the gate so thickly the ground looked like a white pillow with beaks.

"Go away," I started to say. Then it happened.

I heard wings flapping. Then Dusty shouted. At the same second, Kayla screamed. I started to whirl around just as Kayla backed up against me. The latch holding the gate closed snapped.

You can guess what happened next.

Sqwaak! Bock-bock-bock!

I fell over backward on top of the chickens.

CHAPTER TWO

Chicken Wrestling

***Tropical Storm Jacque
Highest Winds—60 m.p.h.***

Sqwaak! Bock-bock-bock!
You'd think with so many feathers, chickens would be soft.

Wrong. They're all lumpy and scratchy, and those beaks and legs are as hard as rocks.

At least the ground was kind of soft and mushy. I was glad for that—for about a half-second. Then I remembered what the ground was probably covered with, since all the chickens were living there. Gross!

Good thing I landed on my back, I thought, happy not to have my face in that stuff. Then the chickens that had flapped up into the air came back down. Two of them tried to land on my face at the same time.

DETECTIVE ZACK

After swatting them away, I opened my eyes and blew the feathers off my face. Most of the chickens had scattered toward the chicken coop, away from us. Kayla was scooting a confused one past me while she looked around nervously. Dusty chased around behind a hen that had escaped, but he was trying harder not to fall down laughing than to catch it.

I sat up and brushed off my arms. "What happened?" I asked, looking around for whatever had sent me into the chicken dust.

Just then, Mr. Tillman stalked up. "What is going on here? Are you trying to kill your grandmother's hens? She'll wring your necks if you do!"

Kayla held up her hands. "Something attacked us! I think it must have been an eagle or a hawk. It came out of nowhere, hit me with its wings, then disappeared again!"

Dusty stopped as Mr. Tillman herded the other chicken back in. "We were just standing here," he tried to explain. "It was an accident that the gate got broken."

"Humph," Mr. Tillman grunted as he wired the gate closed. "Why is it that kids are always having accidents when they're fooling around where they shouldn't be?"

"Let's go," Kayla whispered after we stood there for a second. "He's sure it's our fault. And whatever that was, I don't want to be here if it comes back."

Dusty agreed, and we walked away. "He'll probably tell Grandma we were trying to kill her hens."

"Trying to kill them?" I asked. "I think they were trying to kill me! Did you see them scratching at my eyes? And look at my clothes!"

Dusty wrinkled his nose. "We don't have to look. We can smell them."

While we walked to the house, Dusty was thinking. "What kind of bird would fly right at us and attack us like that?"

"Maybe there was an owl on the ground, and we scared it," I guessed. "Or maybe we got in the way of a hawk that was aiming to have a chicken dinner. Whatever it was, I'm sure we scared it off for good."

Dusty wasn't so sure. "Let's ask Grandpa."

When Dusty and I thundered through the doorway, we almost crashed into his dad. "Slow down there," Uncle Trav said.

"What's going on?" I asked. Everyone was gathered around, staring at the television.

"Shh," he answered. "Listen."

DETECTIVE ZACK

I poked my head between Mom and Grandma. A news reporter was talking. "Next, a report on yesterday's escape from the county jail and an update on a tropical storm that may be headed our way. Right after these commercials."

"Prisoner escape?" Mom asked.

"Tropical storm?" Uncle Trav echoed.

Grandpa shrugged. "I guess I should have been paying more attention to the news." Everyone stared at the screen for a few seconds while a dancing bear tried to sell toilet paper. Then, slowly, their noses crinkled, and their heads turned. Toward me.

"Phew," Grandpa said. "Who's been wrestling with the chickens?"

"All right, all right," I said. "I'll go change. Don't let them start the news again without me!"

By the time I got back, the weather guy was finishing up. ". . . Jacque is moving northwest and is now about 1,250 miles from our shore. With winds up to sixty miles per hour, Tropical Storm Jacque may become a hurricane soon."

"Did he say it was coming this way?" I asked.

"Shh!" everyone said.

"Thanks, Jim," the news reporter said. "The two prisoners who escaped from the county jail have not been found. While these men are not violent criminals, the sheriff reminds us that they are probably desperate and should be considered dangerous. If you see anything suspicious, contact the sheriff's office."

Then Grandpa clicked off the TV, and everyone started talking. "How far away is that jail? Have you seen any strangers today? Have you talked to the sheriff? We'd better lock the doors tonight!"

"Wait a minute!" Dusty spoke louder than anyone else. "What about supper?"

Grandma agreed. "The boy's right. No point in letting supper get cold. I feel sure that this group can eat and talk at the same time." She led the way into the kitchen.

By the time the grown-ups had decided that the criminals wouldn't be heading our way, dark clouds were filling the sky. I remembered what the weather guy had said.

"What is a tropical storm?" I asked. "Is it just a big thunderstorm?"

Uncle Trav shook his head. "It's much bigger. It's called 'tropical' because it forms over the warm waters of the ocean near the equator—that part of the world is called 'the tropics.' "

"It's always warm there, right?"

"Right," he agreed. "Anyway, when the winds are right, a large cluster of storms over the warm

17

water starts to spin like a big whirlpool."

I tried to imagine that. "You mean like the water spins when I flush the toilet?"

Mom groaned. "Zack, not at the supper table." She looked embarrassed. Uncle Trav tried not to laugh.

"Uh, right, I guess. Anyway, as the storms begin to rotate, the winds in the middle get faster and faster. When the storm is spinning, and the winds in the middle are blowing more than thirty-nine miles per hour, meteorologists call it . . ."

"Meteor who?" Dusty interrupted.

"Meteorologists. That's what scientists who study weather are called. Anyway, they call it a tropical storm and give it a name. Like they have this one. What was it? Jenny? Joanie?"

"Jacque [Jackie]," Kayla reminded us.

"How long until it becomes a hurricane?" I asked, listening to the wind in the trees outside the window.

"It may not even get that strong. The winds have to be over seventy-four miles per hour. A lot of tropical storms fizzle out instead of getting stronger."

"Seventy-four!" Dusty almost dropped his fork. "Dad, that's almost as fast as you were driving on the way down here."

"Travis!" Grandma scolded. "I'm sure you know better than to drive that fast."

Now it was Mom's turn to laugh. Uncle Trav turned a little red. "I'm sure I wasn't going that fast," he mumbled.

"Could Tropical Storm Jacque hit Texas while we're here?" I asked. "Right here, where we are?"

"Now, Zack, it's a long, long way away from Texas," Grandpa said. "Not even the weather forecasters know where this storm will go next. Tropical storms and hurricanes sometimes travel in strange paths. We do live close enough to the gulf for hurricanes to be a problem. But it's been more than twenty years since one hit here. I hope this one travels away from us."

I know he's worried about the danger and every-one being safe, but I'm kind of hoping the storm gets closer. Being in a hurricane would be amaz-ing!

Words to Remember

Tropical storm: A storm that forms in the warm waters of the ocean in the tropics. When the storm begins to rotate or spin, and the winds are at least thirty-nine miles per hour.

Hurricane: A tropical storm with winds of at least seventy-four miles per hour.

Meteorologists: Scientists who study weather.

CHAPTER THREE

Strange Light in the Barn

Tropical Storm Jacque
Highest winds—60 m.p.h.

Those dark clouds turned into the thunderstorm that's been keeping me jumping tonight.

Flash! Crash!

"Whoa!" Even Dusty jumped that time. We were up in our room after supper. "That was close! I think it might have hit that big tree out by Millers' barn."

I stood up beside him and stared. "Which one?" While he was pointing, lightning flashed again. Just for a second, it was as bright as day. Then I couldn't see anything at all.

We were still staring out toward the barn when Grandpa came in. "Don't get too close to those windows," he said. "Lightning is a dangerous thing. You boys hungry again yet?"

"Sure," Dusty said as he jumped up. Dusty's always hungry.

"Your grandma's rustling up some popcorn and lemonade," Grandpa added as he turned around. "Come on down if you want to join in." Dusty followed him out the door.

"I'm coming," I called. "I'll be there in just a minute." I just wanted to get a few more things written in my notebook. But by the time I found my pencil, you know what happened.

Flash! Crash! Boom! This time, the lights went out.

When the thunder stopped rolling, I could hear voices from downstairs. I knew they were looking for flashlights and candles. Since my flashlight was in my bag by the bed, I wasn't too worried.

When I bent down to reach for my bag, I looked out toward the old Miller barn again. This time, I could see it. At least I could see one part of it. At the front of the barn closest to the house, a dim light was shining.

That's funny, I thought. *How can there still be electricity in Millers' barn if it's out here in Grandpa's house?*

"Zack! Are you OK up there?"

I was still staring out the window at that light in the barn.

"Zack?"

"I'm fine," I called as I clicked on my flashlight and headed down the stairs. "Grandpa, how can a light be on in the Miller barn if the electricity is out here in the house?"

Grandpa looked up as he struck a match to light a candle. "What? What light in the barn?"

I walked past Dusty and Kayla to a window and stared out. Lightning flashed, and my eyes snapped shut. When I opened them, I couldn't see anything in the darkness. "It was right there," I said, pointing in the direction of the barn. I squinted and kept looking. "Now I don't see any light. But I did. It was either in the doorway or else in that window by the door."

Grandpa lighted the candle, then shook the match out. "I don't know what you saw, Zack, but it couldn't have been a light. Even if the electricity could still be working over there when it isn't over here—and it couldn't—there haven't been any lights in that barn for years."

I whirled around to make sure he wasn't teasing me. By the look on his face, he wasn't. "Then what did I see?" I asked.

Dusty joined me by the window. "Maybe it was

just a reflection."

"Reflection off what?" I asked. "No other lights were on anywhere."

"Maybe it was just your imagination," Kayla suggested with a smile. "Or maybe you're losing your mind."

"Now, now," Grandpa said. "I'm sure Zack saw something. Let's go on to the living room and join the others."

Dusty led the way. "Hey, Zack," he called back, "let's go out there and check it out."

Kayla laughed. "You really have lost your mind if you're thinking about going out in that lightning."

"No one's going anywhere," Mom said firmly from the couch. "Not tonight. Not in this storm."

So we all gathered around the kerosene lantern Grandma set up next to the couch and listened to the storm. "Grandpa," Kayla asked, "this isn't a hurricane, is it?"

"No, no," he answered with a chuckle. "A good hurricane would make this seem like a spring shower. Why, the wind would sound like a hundred freight trains. And the thunder and lightning and rain would go on and on and on."

"But a hurricane could come here?"

"Sure it could," Grandpa said. "When did that

big hurricane blow through here, Grandma? Twenty years ago?"

"More like twenty-five, I think," Grandma said.

Mom nodded. "That's right. I was about your age, Kayla. And Trav was about as old as you two boys."

Uncle Trav smiled. "That was really wild. Remember that old chicken coop? It blew completely away! We picked chickens out of the trees for a week."

"That's when my treehouse tree blew over. I thought the house was going to blow down," Mom added, shaking her head.

"But it didn't," Grandpa stated. "And it won't, even if another hurricane shows up. This is a sturdy old house, and it's been here a long time."

When Uncle Trav launched into another story, Dusty poked me in the arm. "Hey, Zack. Are you thinking what I'm thinking?" he whispered.

I had to think for a minute. "It's time for another snack?"

"No!" Then he tilted his head and thought. "But that is a good idea. What I'm thinking is, maybe you really did see a light in the barn. And maybe it came from those escaped prisoners."

I looked at him. "You might be right. The light I saw was coming from the front of the barn. It could have been right through the open door—you know, the one we kept trying to open last summer?"

"Have you ever been inside that barn?" Dusty asked.

I shook my head. "Have you?"

"No one has," he decided. "Not for a long time."

I tried to remember exactly what I had seen. "The light was dim. It could have been a flashlight. It could have been someone looking for a place to hide." Then another thought hit me. "Maybe those prisoners were hiding in Grandpa's barn this afternoon."

Suddenly, his eyes got so big I could see the whole lantern in each one. "Now I'm thinking what you're thinking! Those sounds we heard could have been them! As soon as it got dark, they must have planned to move on. But the storm made them find another place to hide." He looked around. "Should we tell?"

I shook my head. "Why worry everyone? Besides, we're probably wrong. We'll go check for footprints and clues in the morning." Then I laughed. "Still think there's nothing going on around here?"

His eyes were still big. "Mysterious lights and noises, surprise attacks, escaped prisoners, and maybe a hurricane? And this is just the first day!"

Mystery on the Farm

How could there be a light on in the Miller barn when the electricity was off everywhere? Especially since there haven't been any lights in that barn for a long time!

Could those strange sounds in Grandpa's barn be the escaped prisoners?

What attacked us by the chicken pen?

CHAPTER FOUR

A Mystery About God

Tropical Storm Jacque
Winds—70 m.p.h.

By this time, the thunderstorm was fading into the distance. "We might as well go on to bed," Grandpa said. "The power's liable to be out till morning."

So I wrote by flashlight in my bed. And even if that house was full of scratching sounds as loud as the ones we heard in the barn, I couldn't have heard them. Dusty's snoring blocked out everything else. I still couldn't see anything outside the window, so whatever I saw in Millers' barn was gone.

I finally got a few words written. It's great to be at Grandpa's, especially since Dusty's here. Usually, our whole family makes a trip to Texas to visit our grandparents every summer. We meet Dusty and his family there, and it's a great week of family fun.

But this time is different. Only my mom and Kayla and I came, and Dusty and his dad, Uncle Trav. The big old farmhouse seems kind of empty. Especially since Aunt Nina isn't here. She's my mom's and Dusty's dad's sister. Or I guess I should say, she was.

Aunt Nina died last spring. And that's really why we're here. We came to the funeral back then, but Mom said that she wanted to come back. "I just want to get together with my mother and father and brother and spend some time remembering Nina," she said. Dad couldn't get away from work for that long, so he stayed home with Alex.

But I'm here, and I'm remembering Aunt Nina too. She was my favorite aunt. She wasn't married and didn't have any kids to play with, but she was great. Whenever we wanted to go somewhere to have fun, she wanted to take us. Whenever we started up a game, she joined in.

Maybe it was because she's known me the longest (I'm the oldest nephew), but I think she liked me best. She never forgot my birthday. And she wrote me a letter or a card almost every month. She was the greatest!

But now she's gone.

And I guess that's why I'm writing in this notebook. I've filled up several notebooks writing down things that help show that the Bible is true—things like rocks that tell the story of the Flood, and dug-up cities that support the Bible stories. I found plenty of reasons to believe in the Bible and in God.

But now it's not so easy to believe.

When Aunt Nina got sick, we all prayed for her. Dad read a verse in the Bible that said, "Ask, and you will receive." He read about other people in the Bible who were sick but God healed them. We prayed a lot, for a long time.

Aunt Nina died anyway.

If God is real, and He really cares about us, why did He let Aunt Nina die? What good does praying do? It didn't help Aunt Nina.

I asked my mom about it on the way down here. "Mom, why didn't God answer our prayers about Aunt Nina?"

She sighed and looked really sad. "Maybe He did," she said. "Maybe He just said No."

"I don't think I understand."

She sighed and looked at me. "Zack, it's very hard for most people to understand. Some people

33

think it's one of the greatest mysteries about God."

That sounded interesting. "A mystery?"

She nodded. "Maybe it's something you could explore. You might not solve the mystery, but you might understand it better."

So that's why I'm writing in my notebook this time. I want to find out if there are any reasons to believe what the Bible says about praying. I wish there was somewhere I could look or clues I could find, but I don't know where or what.

The best clue would have been if Aunt Nina had gotten better.

At first this morning, I didn't know what woke me up. *It must have been Old Red Top*, I decided, without opening my eyes. *That rooster always has to get up before the sun does.*

Then I heard it again.

Err—erer-eroo!

I smiled. *That's Old Red Top all right.* I was almost asleep when the rooster started crowing again.

Errr—erer—aack!

This time, one of my eyes popped open. It was just barely light outside, but it still hurt. At the same moment, Dusty sat up in his bed. "What in the world was that?" he muttered.

"It sounded like someone strangled the rooster," I answered. Dusty groaned and crawled back under his covers. I guess I did the same thing, because the next thing I knew, the sun was beaming straight into my eyes. From the voices coming up the stairs, I knew everyone else was already awake.

"It didn't bother me a bit. I slept right through the whole storm."

"Not Sonia again," Dusty groaned. "Make her go away." By the time we got dressed and found our way to the kitchen, she and Kayla were on their second stack of pancakes.

"Good morning, boys," Grandma said. "The electricity is back on, and breakfast is ready. Looks like the smell of pancakes woke you up."

"Not exactly," Dusty mumbled, glaring at Sonia. But that didn't stop him from sliding into a chair and reaching for the syrup.

"Sonia," Grandma asked, "how's Oreo? You haven't brought your rabbit over lately."

"You have a rabbit?" Kayla asked. "Can I come see it?"

"No," Sonia answered. "I had to get rid of it."

"Too bad." Kayla frowned under her milk mustache. "I like rabbits."

Sonia nodded sadly. "So do I. But my dad doesn't.

He said there are enough rabbits around here without adding more."

By that time, after a few bites and a glass of cold milk, I was ready to start thinking. "Has anyone been outside this morning?"

"I have," Sonia said through a mouthful of food. "I walked over here, after all. And your grandpa was out at the hay barn checking to see if anything was broken by the storm last night."

"Mom and I walked up to the Miller barn before breakfast," Kayla added. "We didn't see anything broken around there."

"Great," I muttered. "You know what that means," I whispered to Dusty.

Dusty stopped chewing. "What?" The look on his face reminded me that he wakes up even slower than I do.

"Clues," I reminded him. "Clues about that light in the barn last night. And those sounds yesterday."

Slowly, Dusty caught on. "Should we go look now?" He stared sadly at the rest of his pancakes.

"No hurry now," I said. "Everyone's already been out there, tramping all over the place. There probably aren't any clues left anyway."

I finished eating first (big surprise, knowing Dusty's appetite), so I walked to Grandpa's barn and climbed to the loft to wait for Dusty. Just being out there alone made me think of Aunt Nina. She used to play up there with us a lot. When I heard noises down below, I hung my head down through the hatch hole. "Oh, hi, Grandma. I thought you were Dusty."

"No, no, it's just me, checking on my chickens. Thank the Lord, the storm didn't do any damage out here."

"Grandma," I asked, "do you really believe God kept the storm from breaking anything?"

"Well, Zack, I prayed and asked Him to watch over our farm."

I climbed down the ladder and sat on a hay bale. "Why do you still pray after Aunt Nina died? It seems like God didn't answer your prayer then. He didn't answer any of our prayers."

Before she could answer, a sound from the yard made both of our heads swivel around. Someone screamed!

Prayer Clues

The Bible says, "Ask, and it will be given to you." What if you don't get what you ask for? Is the Bible wrong?

Why did Aunt Nina die, when we all prayed for her to get well?

CHAPTER FIVE

Grown-ups and God

Tropical Storm Jacque
Winds—70 m.p.h.

Grandma was headed for the door before the screaming even stopped. I was right behind her. I already knew who was screaming—it had to be Kayla.

It was. She was huddled down by the chicken pen. Dusty was hiding behind a tree. "It attacked me again!" Kayla shouted. "We were just walking out to the barn to find you guys and . . ."

"Wait a minute," Grandma interrupted. "What attacked you?" She was already helping Kayla up and checking to see if she was hurt. "Are you OK?"

Kayla stood up easily. "I'm fine. It just scared me."

"Was it the thing with wings?" I asked. "Just like last time"?

"Just like last time," Dusty answered. "It flew right at us. Then it disappeared into the woods."

"Wait a minute!" Grandma almost shouted. "What do you mean 'last time?' This has happened to you before? Someone start telling me what's going on!"

"We were going to tell Grandpa last night," I said quickly. "But the storm made me forget." We told her about my experience with her chickens. She's such a nice grandmother she didn't even laugh. Or maybe she was just worried about her chickens. "We thought it might be a hawk or an owl. But I didn't think it would come back."

"You're not going to believe this," Dusty said, "but it looked like—a chicken!"

I didn't believe it. "A chicken? You mean, like a wild one that attacks people?" I looked over the fence at the flock of clucking, pecking feather brains. "You've got to be kidding."

"Don't be so sure about that," Grandma said. "Not all chickens are fat and lazy like these white leghorns. I'd better get to the bottom of this. Is there anything else you were going to tell us?"

I tried to remember. "Well, I think I heard something strange this morning. It was early, just when it was getting light. I heard Old Red Top crow; then he started to crow again, and it sounded like someone choked him!"

"Oh yeah," Dusty agreed. Then he frowned. "I thought I dreamed that."

Maybe because of all the commotion or because he was getting impatient for his food, Old Red Top appeared from behind the chicken coop. *Errr—erer—eroo!* he crowed.

Before any of us could say a word, a answer came from the nearest tree. *Errr—erer—aack!*

"What in the world?" Kayla asked as she ducked down.

Dusty's mouth dropped open. "That's exactly what we heard! Right, Zack?"

Grandma shook her head. "Lucifer," she muttered. "I should have known."

My eyebrows went straight up. "Who?"

Before she answered, a large brown bird dived to the ground just in front of us. Everyone but Grandma took a step back. "It's a—a rooster!" Dusty announced.

"That's right," Grandma said as the rooster strutted back and forth. Its brown feathers flashed red and gold in the sunlight. "It's Mr. Tillman's Bantam rooster. We call him Lucifer because he's as pretty as an angel but as mean as a devil."

Kayla took another step back. "Is he dangerous?

Grandma nodded. "He could be, but I think he's just trying to scare us. Bantam roosters have spurs, sharp claws at the back of their feet, and they can be trained to fight. Bantams are good fliers and are quick and naturally aggressive. That means they will easily attack other roosters or anything that comes into their territory."

"So what's he doing here?" Dusty asked. "This isn't his territory."

"That's a good question," Grandma answered. "I'm sure he's here wanting to fight Old Red Top and take over my chickens. The question is, why isn't Mr. Tillman keeping him in his pen at home? As soon as I'm finished with my chickens, I'll try to find out."

Dusty and I followed Grandma into the barn to help. She headed straight toward a door I had never seen open. "Dusty, what's in that room?" I asked.

He shrugged. "I've never been in there. Why?"

"Do you think it's big enough for someone to hide in? Maybe two people?"

His eyes almost popped out. "Those prisoners! If they are hiding in this barn, they might be in that room! Do you think we should have told her that too?"

There was no time to answer. Grandma was reaching for the door. "Uh, Grandma, wait for us! We'll help you." I raced up and grabbed the bucket from her hand. Dusty grabbed the doorknob and held the door closed.

"Well, thank you," Grandma said. "You're both being very polite—all of a sudden." The look on her face reminded me of Mom when she's sure I'm up to something.

Dusty took a deep breath and slowly pulled the door open. "Here we are," he said in a loud voice. I stepped into the doorway right behind him and stuck my head in to look around. The room was dark and nearly empty. There were some suspicious-looking lumps in one corner, though.

"Wouldn't it be easier to see with the light on?" Grandma asked as she reached in and flipped the switch. I cringed, but the lumps in the corner didn't jump up. They just lay there like the bags of chicken feed they were.

Grandma stepped past me. "It's just a storage room, boys. Most hay barns have one or two. We used to store cattle feed in here. Fertilizer was kept in the next room. Oh, Dusty, will you go get the hose and bring it to the chicken pen? We need to refill their water dishes too."

After he left, Grandma picked up a half-empty bag of feed. "I thought this bag was nearly full," she said to herself. After she filled the bucket I was holding, I turned to head out. But she put her hand on my shoulder. "Zack, do you remember what I gave you for Christmas last year?"

"Sure." I reached into my pocket and pulled out my pocketknife. "It's a great knife. I've used it lots of times. And I've been very careful."

"I'm sure you have," she said with a smile. "But do you remember how much your little brother wanted one?"

I remembered, all right. Alex almost threw a fit! He didn't want the tool set he unwrapped—he wanted a knife. "Why can't I have one?" he begged. "I'll be careful. I promise!"

"He sure did want one," I answered. "But he didn't get one."

She smiled. "He was sure that he was big enough to have a knife, and he was sure he wouldn't get hurt using it. He just knew that he should have a knife. He was wrong, but he wasn't grown up enough to know it."

I thought about that. "Like if I wanted to go drive Mom's car. At least I'm grown up enough to know that I'm not grown up enough to do that."

Grandma nodded. "Sometimes, I think it's that

way with God. I was very sure that the best thing for Nina was that she get well. But to God, I'm even more of a child than Alex is."

I had to smile about that. If Grandma is like a child, God must be really old.

She went on. "God is wiser, more grown up than I am. If He could see that allowing Nina to die was all right, then I can either throw a fit like Alex, or I can trust Him." She was quiet for moment, and I could see a tear roll down her cheek. "For a while, I did throw a fit. I shouted at God and cried. And I still miss Nina very much every day. But I'm trying to be grown up enough to know that I'm not grown up enough to know everything God knows. I've decided to trust God, even though I don't understand why."

That gave me a lot to think about. I mean, I've thought of God as my Father in heaven, but I never really thought of him as a dad. I guess if Mom and Dad know what's best for a little kid like Alex, maybe God knows what's best for the rest of us.

Well, the mysterious attack didn't turn out to be much of a mystery—just a rooster who thinks he owns the wrong place. Maybe the other mystery isn't real either. Maybe I didn't really see a light in Millers' barn. Maybe those escaped prisoners are nowhere near here. Maybe the noises we heard was that crazy rooster. Maybe there's nothing going on at all.

Maybe.

Prayer Clues

Grandma says God is much more grown up than even she is, and much wiser. So either we can throw a fit when things happen that we don't understand, or we can trust Him. She's decided to trust Him.

If moms and dads know what's best for little kids, maybe God knows what's best for the rest of us.

Mystery in the Barn

Some mystery! Just a crazy rooster who attacked us by the chicken pen.

Words to Remember

White leghorns: Nice white-feathered chickens like Grandma's.

Bantams: Smaller, beautiful brown-gold-and-red chickens. Roosters have spurs, sharp claws at the back of their feet, and they can be trained to fight. Bantams are good fliers and are quick and naturally aggressive.

CHAPTER SIX

Clues
in the Barn

Tropical Storm Jacque
Winds—70 m.p.h.

Now I know I was wrong. Something is going on. Kayla and Dusty and I finally searched for clues after lunch. But first we heard the noon weather report.

The meteorologist was standing in front of a map of the Gulf of Mexico. Mostly, he stood in front of Texas, so I couldn't find the spot where Grandma and Grandpa's farm is. "Tropical Storm Jacque is getting stronger every hour," he reported. "You can see the swirl of clouds here, just entering the gulf. Wind speeds are now up to seventy miles per hour, and we expect them to get stronger. Folks, Jacque will soon be a hurricane. If you live near the gulf coast, stay tuned for the latest developments. Our next update will be on tonight's news."

"We'd better tune in," Grandpa said. "But it's still a long way away."

Grandma surprised us with a scoop of ice cream for desert. "Thanks for helping me with the chickens, boys. "

"You're welcome," Dusty said with a grin. "Grandma, those chickens really are valuable, aren't they? I mean, they win all those blue ribbons and everything."

Grandma smiled. "Yes, I suppose they are. But that's not why I keep them. They're certainly more trouble than they are worth. Still, I enjoy fussing with them and seeing the new ones grow. And eating the eggs," she added with a wink. "They're almost like pets to me now. Taking them to the fair is just for fun. But don't tell Mr. Tillman I said that!"

That puzzled me. "Doesn't he take his chickens to the fair too?"

"Oh yes," Grandma answered. "And he's very serious about winning the blue ribbon. It upsets him every year when my hens win and his don't."

Dusty poked me in the arm. "Zack, are we still going to look for clues in the barn?" he whispered.

"I guess so." I tried to sound interested. "Even

though no strangers were hiding in the feed room this morning, that doesn't mean no one was there last night. We need to go back and look for footprints—if we didn't wipe them out this morning."

"This is my footprint," I said as Dusty, Kayla, and I walked into the feed room. "See?" I placed an identical new print by the old one.

"Here's mine," Dusty reported.

"Is this one Grandma's?" Kayla asked. We decided that it was.

"Now, let's look for any prints that look different," I said.

"Here's one," Kayla called. Then her face turned red. "Oops, that's my shoe. Never mind." She changed the subject. "Zack, why is there a slide in here?"

At one side of the room was something I hadn't seen this morning. It was a kind of a wooden slide that led up to a slot in the wall. "Why would someone build a playground in a feed room?" I wondered.

A voice from the doorway laughed. It was Grandpa. "Zack, that's not a slide. At least, it's not one for people. Back when we had cows on this farm, we kept a lot of bags of cattle feed in here. That slide made it easier to unload those bags. Your dad, Dusty, would take the bags off the truck and slide them through a slot in the barn wall. Then I'd catch them down here and stack them in the corner."

I climbed partway up the slide. "Where's the slot? I can't see outside."

"I nailed a cover over it to keep the rats out." He went over to the bags of feed and counted. Then he frowned. "You kids haven't been feeding the chickens any extra food, have you?"

"Just what we fed them with Grandma this morning," I answered. "Why?"

"Grandma mentioned that the bag was more empty than she thought. Now that I count them, it seems we're missing a whole bag. It's very strange. Well, ya'll be careful." He left with a wave, and we went back to looking for clues.

"What about this print?" Dusty asked. "It's different." He was right. It had a big round circle in the heel.

"Just a second," I said. I ran to the doorway and looked for Grandpa's print. "No, it's not his boot. And I don't think Mom or Uncle Trav has been out here. So a stranger has been in this room. We'd better check for clues at the old Miller barn."

When we got there, I rattled the lock on the big bar across the door. "I thought maybe the light was coming through the door, like the door was open. But I guess that's not true. It looks like this door hasn't been open in years."

"Too bad we can't get inside," Dusty said. He leaned over and tried to fit his face past the bars that protected the window next to the door. "Do you think the light could have come from here?"

"It must have," I agreed, crowding up next to him. "Can you see anything at all?" We both shielded our eyes with our hands, but it didn't help much.

"All I can see is a dark room," Dusty said. He shook his head. "Zack, are you sure you saw a light? I mean, it could have been lightning reflecting or something."

"Maybe you're right." I shook my head. "Maybe I'm imagining the whole thing."

"Hey, if someone was here with a light, then they had to leave footprints," Kayla reminded us. "We could see Mom's and my footprints from this morning when we walked up here. Let's walk around the barn."

We walked slowly so we wouldn't miss anything or step on any good prints. "Wait a minute," I said before we were halfway around. "This is a waste of time. The rain last night washed out any footprints that might have been here."

Dusty collapsed against the barn wall. Then he

looked up. "Hey, look at that board nailed to the wall. Do you think this barn has a slot like Grandpa's?" He reached up and pulled on one edge of the old board. It broke into two pieces and fell to the ground. That left a wide slot showing in the barn wall. "Whoa! I guess it does. There must be a feed-storage room down there too. Want to slide down and see?"

Kayla and I crowded up close as Dusty stuck his head inside the slot. "Hello, down there," he called. Then he pulled his head back. "Whew! That's a strong smell. And not a nice one."

I sniffed, and my nose wrinkled. He was right about that. "Can you hear anything?" I asked. We both turned our heads to listen.

Dusty frowned. "I don't—wait a minute. Do you hear scratching?"

I did hear it. "It sounds kind of like what we heard in the barn yesterday."

"Rats!" Kayla shouted. We both looked at her. "It must be rats—lots of rats. I wouldn't go down there for anything. Let's go."

When we got around to the end of the barn with the big wooden doors, I was ready to give up. "Even these big doors are barred closed," Dusty pointed out. "And they've been closed a long time. Look—this was probably just a little tree when

56

the Millers lived here. Now it's as tall as the barn, and it's got branches right in front of the doors."

While he went over to try to peek through the crack of the two big doors, I walked around the tree. I almost stepped on some old footprints before I saw them. "Look," I said to Kayla, "these aren't completely washed out. Do you think they look like the ones with the big circle?"

She bent down to study them. "They might be the same. It's hard to tell with all those raindrop marks."

"Hey!" Dusty called. He was excited. "You've got to see this!"

We raced over and peeked through the doors. And from the dim light coming through the dust-covered windows, we could see them.

Footprints. Lots of them, in the dust on the wooden floor.

Mystery in the Barn

We found footprints in the feed room that didn't match anyone's in our family.

Millers' barn is locked up tight, but there are footprints inside!

Millers' barn has a feed chute like Grandpa's. Are those strange sounds down there like the ones we heard in Grandpa's barn?

The footprints under the tree might be the same as the one in the feed room.

CHAPTER SEVEN

Two Ideas, Two Suspects

Tropical Storm Jacque
Winds—70 m.p.h.

"We've got to look at all the clues," I told the others when we got back to Grandpa's hayloft. "Let's make a list."

"OK," Kayla said. "We know that someone has been inside the Miller barn. So you must have really seen that light during the storm."

"Right," I said as I wrote it down. "Also, we know that someone besides family has been in the feed room here."

Dusty thought for a second. "We know that Lucifer is loose. He could have made the noises we heard. Remember, Sonia said that noises in a barn can seem extra loud."

"You don't think he'd come up here, do you?"

Kayla asked, looking around. "He really gets on my nerves."

I ignored her. "So it looks like the escaped prisoners hid in this barn in the feed room, then left as soon as it got dark. Because of the storm, they hid in the Miller barn."

"But, Zack, how did they get in?" Kayla asked. "None of the doors had been opened. None of the windows were open or broken. Even the feed chute had a board nailed over it."

"And are they still there?" Dusty asked. "If they left after the storm, we should have seen their footprints."

I frowned. "OK, but what else could be going on?"

Kayla snapped her fingers. "We forgot something. Didn't Grandpa say that chicken feed is missing?"

I wrote it down while I thought out loud. "Why would anyone around here want chicken feed? The only ones with chickens are . . ." While I was saying it, something hit me. "Hey, didn't Grandma say that Mr. Tillman is really jealous of her prize-winning chickens?"

Kayla whirled around. "You don't think he would be stealing feed from Grandma and Grandpa, do you? He works for them."

I waved my hand. "What if he's really mad

about her winning every year? What if he set Lucifer free on purpose, hoping he would get into her chicken pen and fight with Old Red Top? What if he's trying to mess up her chickens before the fair next month?"

They were both quiet for a minute. Then Dusty said, "He certainly would be able to get in here without any problem. He's in this barn almost every day."

Kayla shook her head. "I still don't think Sonia's dad would do that."

Then we heard a voice shouting across the yard. "OK, I'll look in the loft." It was Sonia.

"What do we tell her?" Kayla hissed.

"Nothing about any of this," I said. By the time Sonia climbed up the ladder, we had the big doors pushed back and were sitting there with our feet hanging over the edge.

"Hi, guys," she called. "What are you up to?"

"Nothing much," Kayla answered. "Just staring at the old Miller barn and wishing something was happening here."

Sonia sat down beside her. "Yeah, really. You guys being here is about the only interesting thing that's happened all summer."

"You don't think a hurricane would be interesting?" Dusty asked.

Sonia shrugged. "Sure, but it never happens. There hasn't been one here since I was born. Sometimes they come close, but they always turn at the last minute."

"Mom said there was one about twenty-five years ago," Kayla said. "So they do happen sometimes."

"It must not have been a very strong one," Sonia responded. "After all, this barn wasn't damaged."

"Neither was Millers' barn," I guessed. "They must both be built the same." Something about that tickled my brain, but it slipped away before I could grab it.

"Mom's praying that Tropical Storm Jacque will miss us," Kayla said.

Sonia snorted. "Praying? Dad says praying is for people who can't take care of themselves."

"You don't believe in praying? Or in God?" I asked.

She shook her head. "I believe there is a God. I guess I just don't believe He really cares about what happens to us. I mean, what happens if He answers your mom's prayer and the storm heads a different way? Then someone else prays, so He has to change it again. Where does it finally go? Where no one prays?"

No one had an answer to that.

Two Ideas, Two Suspects

Sonia went on. "What if your mom prays that it goes somewhere else, and I pray that it comes here? Never mind, I know what happens. My prayers never get answered."

Listening to Sonia gave me something to think about. After all, how does God decide whose prayer to answer? Maybe God is there, but He doesn't really care about what happens to us.

At supper, Grandma was talking about Lucifer. "I talked to Mr. Tillman about that rooster. He says Lucifer got out accidentally last week, and he's been looking for him every day since then."

"I guess he was happy to know that we found him," Grandpa said.

"Yes, but he wasn't sure that the rooster could be caught out in the open. He's hoping to lure it back inside his pen." Grandma frowned. "I'm afraid Lucifer will get into our pen and cause trouble."

I raised my fork. "Grandma, could we try to catch him for you? I'm sure we could outsmart that rooster." Dusty nodded with his mouth full.

Grandma thought for a second. "I don't think Mr. Tillman could object to that. What do you have in mind?"

I grinned. "We'll set a trap!"

Kayla groaned. "Oh no. I know how Zack's traps turn out."

"Don't listen to her, Grandma. My traps always work. Well, almost always."

After supper, we agreed to keep an eye on the Miller barn. "We can solve this right away if a light comes on out there again," I said. "We'll race down there and see who's home."

I took my turn first, so while Kayla and Dusty sat in front of the television, I sat in a chair facing the window and pretended to read a book. Since I was just pretending, I had plenty of time to think about what Sonia said about prayer. When Grandpa walked by, I had a question.

"Grandpa, what does God do when one person prays for something to happen, and another person prays for it not to happen?"

Grandpa sat in the chair next to mine. "Zack, tell me about a time when you wanted the family to do one thing and Kayla wanted the family to do something else."

That didn't take long. "Just last weekend. I wanted to go to the park, where all of us could play a game. Kayla wanted us to go to the mall and go shopping." I looked at him. "How did you know we wanted to do different things?"

He laughed. "Believe me, I know. Brothers and sisters grew up in this house too. Anyway, Zack, how did your parents decide what to do?"

I had to think about that. I knew what we did—we went to the park. But why did they decide to do what I wanted?

Grandpa asked it again. "I know that they love both of you the same and that they wanted to make each of you happy. So how did they decide?"

Slowly, I remembered. "Dad said the family would get more exercise in the park than from just walking through the mall. He said it would be better for all of us."

"I think God works the same way," Grandpa said. "Sometimes He can do whatever a person needs or wants. Sometimes, He looks at what's going on and decides that something else would be better for that person. And sometimes He does what is best for the family—the whole human family."

That made sense.

Grandpa went on. "I think God cares about each person, but He sees things no one else can see. He knows what's going to happen. And most of all, He wants to put an end to this world of sin and take us all to heaven, where no one will get sick or die."

After Grandpa left, I kept thinking. But before I could decide whether or not he was right, Dusty started shouting my name.

"Zack, get in here! You have to hear this."

DETECTIVE ZACK

I ran into the living room in time to hear the newsperson say, "Now to the weather, where Jim has some big news."

"It's big news, all right," the man in front of the map said. "It's a big storm. With wind speeds of eighty miles per hour, Jacque is now a hurricane. The forecast is for her to continue along the same path, which brings the storm directly toward the Texas coast."

Prayer Clues

Sonia's dad says praying is for people who can't take care of themselves. Could that be true?

Sonia doesn't believe that God really cares about what happens to us. She has a good question: How does God decide whose prayer to answer? Maybe God is there, but He doesn't really care about what happens to us.

Grandpa says that God is like a parent. Sometimes He can do whatever a person needs or wants. But sometimes, He has to decide what's best for a person—or what's best for the whole human family.

Mystery in the Barn

Someone was inside the Miller barn! So I really did see a light during the storm.

Someone besides family has been in Grandpa's feed room.

Lucifer could have made the noises we heard in Grandpa's barn.

Chicken feed is missing from the feed room.

Idea Number One: The escaped prisoners hid in Grandpa's feed room, then hid in the Miller barn because of the storm.

But there are no clues about how they could have gotten inside and no prints to show that they left again.

Idea Number Two: Maybe Mr. Tillman is really jealous because Grandma's chickens win the blue ribbon every year. Maybe he's trying to mess up her chances of winning at the fair next month?

CHAPTER EIGHT

Freedom and a Trap

Hurricane Jacque
Winds—79 m.p.h.

"What is the most important thing in the universe?"

I didn't know the answer to that question yesterday. And I haven't had time to write down a thing since then. But now Dusty's asleep, and the electricity is on—which is a good thing, since my flashlight batteries are nearly dead. So I turned on the lamp by my bed, and I'm going to get something written down—while I keep an eye on the Miller barn.

When we first sat down in church yesterday, I wasn't paying attention very well. Aunt Nina's funeral was in this church. It was filled with crying and sad, quiet voices. I guess I expected it to stay that way, because the smiles and laughing surprised me.

One thing was the same—the purple flowers. Aunt Nina brought those flowers every week for church, and for her funeral, they filled the church with purple flowers.

The church smelled just as I remembered it—like purple flowers. But instead of making me sad, this time it made me smile.

Since I wasn't paying attention, I was surprised again. When it was time for the preacher to preach, Grandpa stood up!

"Pastor Vinson can't be with us every week at our little church, and this week he asked me to fill in. So I want to start with a question: What is the most important thing in the universe?

"Now I know that love, God's love, is the most powerful force. Because of that love, Jesus was willing to do the most astounding thing anyone could imagine. He came and died for us. And He did it to preserve the most important thing in the universe—freedom."

That surprised me. Is freedom really that important?

Grandpa went on. "When God created humans, He created them with a free will. That means He gave them the ability to choose and the freedom to do it. Even though He knew that they could choose to do wrong, to hurt themselves. Freedom was so important, He gave it to humans, even though He knew they might choose to hate Him. Because only if we are free to hate Him can we truly choose to love Him."

Grandpa looked right at me. "Freedom is the most important thing in the universe. But look at what God gives up because of our freedom! Sometimes we choose to do things that hurt us—He has to let us choose. Sometimes we choose to do things that hurt others—He has to let us choose. Because we live in a sinful world, sometimes bad things just happen."

I knew he was talking about Aunt Nina.

"Because He gave us the freedom to choose, God can't always step in and stop pain and sickness and death. But He does better than that. He has a plan that will allow us to choose to live forever in peace and happiness. He gives us the chance to choose to live with Him in heaven."

If Grandpa's right, then when God gave us freedom, He gave up some of His. He can't step in with miracles all the time. But sometimes He does! I wonder how He decides when to do miracles?

And I wonder how He answers prayers when He decides He can't do a miracle.

DETECTIVE ZACK

Grandpa clicked on the TV during breakfast this morning. "We'd better keep up with that storm, just in case," he said.

"With Hurricane Jacque churning up the gulf, let's get the latest update from Jim, our meteorologist. The storm is already affecting our weather. Jim, is it coming here?"

While they chattered, I looked out the window. The trees were twisting as the wind came in big puffs. Dark clouds raced by overhead.

"We can expect gusty winds and occasional showers today," Jim announced. "But Hurricane Jacque should continue on a course that will take it west of us. Anyone along the coast should keep up to the minute with the forecast. Jacque's winds will create high waves and coastal flooding. But for the folks inland, I think we'll just see the edges of the storm."

After breakfast, we decided it was time to catch Lucifer. "What we need is a trap," I announced.

"Uh-oh," Kayla warned, "when he says that, look out!"

Dusty looked at her. "What do you mean? Zack's not making a trap to catch us."

"Then I hope it doesn't," Kayla said with a laugh. Dusty still looked confused.

You can count on a sister to be that way. Just

because a few of my best traps have backfired and caught the wrong people, she has to remind me and everyone else about the ones that went wrong. What about the ones that worked, after all?

"It's not even that kind of trap," I said with a glare. "This a very simple trap. Nothing could possibly go wrong. We'll just catch Lucifer and take him to Mr. Tillman."

Dusty liked that. "So this is a trap like the ones forest rangers use."

"Not exactly," I had to tell him.

"What exactly is it?" Kayla asked.

I pointed to the wooden crate my foot was on and pulled some string from behind my back. "I told you it was very simple. All we need now is a stick to prop the crate up, some bait, and a board to close him in when we catch him."

Dusty moaned. "Are you sure this will work?"

By the time we had the trap set up in the woods, I almost had them convinced. "Now all we have to do is hide down in this gully and hold on to the string. If Lucifer is hiding out here somewhere, that chicken-feed bait will lure him in. Then we'll pull the string, yank out the stick, and presto! The rooster will be our prisoner."

Even Kayla had to admit it was a good plan. "Only a few things could go wrong: the rooster might not be hiding in these woods, and it might not go in the trap. And we might sit out here all day for nothing. But at least I don't see any way it could backfire and get us into trouble."

I won't bother you with how boring it was to sit there quietly for hours, trying to be quiet. But finally, Kayla whispered, "I see something moving toward the trap!"

"Is it the rooster?" Dusty and I both tried to see what she was seeing.

"I can't tell," she hissed. "All I can see are the leaves of the bushes moving. Just pull that string when I saw so." After a few more tense seconds, she said it. "Pull!"

I yanked the string, and we heard the crate fall with a thud. "We got it!" Dusty cried.

"See, I told you," I had to say. "No problems at all." Kayla led the way to the crate. But she stopped so suddenly I ran right into her.

"Zack!" she hissed. "Can you see between the slats?"

I stared. Whatever was in there was moving around in circles. That was OK, but something else was wrong. Very wrong.

"Come on," Dusty said. "Let's go get it."

"I don't think so," Kayla replied. "Even from here, I can tell that's not a rooster under that crate. It's an animal. And it has black-and-white fur."

Dusty looked blank. I tried to help as I began to back away. "What kind of animal has black-and-white fur? You know, black with a white stripe, maybe?"

His eyes got big again. But he didn't back away. He turned and ran!

Prayer Clues

Did God give up some of His freedom when He gave us ours? If He did, then He can't always step in and do miracles. He created people with the freedom to choose and to experience what happens when they choose the wrong things.

How does He decides when to do miracles?

How does He answer prayers when He decides He can't do a miracle?

_____

_____

_____

_____

_____

_____

_____

_____

_____

_____

_____

_____

_____

_____

_____

_____

_____

_____

CHAPTER NINE

Mistake in the Crate

Hurricane Jacque
Winds—94 m.p.h.

For a second, I wanted to run right after Dusty. I mean, would you want to hang around a crate that was holding an unhappy skunk?

But I didn't. "Dusty! Wait a minute. I don't smell anything. Maybe the skunk isn't mad yet."

He stopped. "Maybe not yet. But it will be."

"We can't just run off and leave it there," Kayla insisted. "We have to at least let it loose."

"She's right," I said. "Come on, let's figure something out." We crept back to hide behind a tree that wasn't too far from the crate—or too close. "It must not be too mad," I said, sniffing the air. "Maybe we can tip the crate over."

Dusty agreed. "I'll look for a long stick. If I can

find one, we can try to tip it without getting too close." Before long, he had pulled the twigs off a long branch from a dead tree.

"Great," I said. "Now, who's going to tip it?" I asked. They both stared at me. "OK, OK, I'll do it." I slipped slowly and silently around the tree and began walking toward the crate. A stick snapped under my foot.

"Shh!" someone whispered from behind the tree.

I finally got close enough to slide the branch across a rock. Then I took a deep breath and slipped the end under one corner of the crate. My plan was simple. I'd shove down on the branch, and the crate would pop up. Before it even hit the ground, I'd be back behind the tree.

I wanted to give the skunk time to calm down. "One, two, three . . ." When I got to ten, I shoved the branch down hard!

Right away, three things went wrong. The branch snapped in half right under my hand! Since I wasn't expecting that, I lurched forward! My foot hit the rock, and I tripped!

All of this left me on my face, two feet from the crate. I looked up into two beady little eyes and realized something.

"Hey, this isn't a skunk. It's a rabbit!" I crawled

closer and peered between the slats. "It's one of those black-and-white ones, like people keep for pets."

Kayla rushed over. "Aw, it's cute! Can we keep it?"

"Didn't Grandma say that Sonia had a pet rabbit?" Dusty asked. "I wonder if this is hers?"

Kayla slipped her fingers through and tried to pet the rabbit. It kicked up its heels and retreated as far away as it could. "It doesn't act like a pet."

Dusty and I slipped the board underneath the crate and picked it up, rabbit and all. We met Grandma out in the yard. "A rabbit? I don't think we want to keep a wild animal as a pet. They belong out in the woods."

"But, Grandma," Kayla pleaded, "this isn't a wild rabbit. At least, it's not supposed to be. Look!"

When Grandma saw the black-and-white animal, she was puzzled too. "What is that rabbit doing in our woods?"

"You don't think it's Sonia's pet?" Dusty asked.

She looked again. "Well, it's the same kind of rabbit. But I'm sure Sonia's was bigger. And both of its ears were black."

Our captured rabbit wiggled its black ear and its white ear and stayed as far from us as possible. "What are we going to do with it?" I asked.

DETECTIVE ZACK

"Well, let's put it in the barn for now," she suggested. "Grandpa has an old cage out there that should do for a temporary home."

We hosed the wire cage clean, then tried to scoot Black and White into it. "Ow!" Dusty said when the rabbit toenail scraped his hand. "He sure doesn't act like he's ever been around people."

When we finally got him in the cage, Grandma suggested we put it in the feed room. "What should we feed him?" Kayla asked.

"Pull some grass to put in his cage," Grandma answered. "And I'm sure he'd like a handful of chicken feed. Just be sure he can't get out of that cage. He'd have holes chewed in those bags of feed in no time."

Kayla stayed to talk to the rabbit and "try to tame it." I went to find Mom to tell her what we caught in my trap.

"Mom?" I called, knocking on the door of her room. It wasn't really her room. It was Aunt Nina's while she lived with my grandparents, but that's where Mom was sleeping.

"Come in, Zack," she called. I told her about almost catching a skunk but catching a rabbit instead. After we laughed, I asked, "Mom, does being in this room make you feel sad?"

She sat at the desk and stared out the window.

The branches of the tree just outside swayed back and forth in the wind. "Not always sad, at least not anymore. Everything here reminds me of her. I miss her, but the memories I have are very happy."

I sniffed the flowers on Aunt Nina's desk. "This smell always reminds me of her," I said to Mom. "Even in church it did."

"Me too," she said.

That reminded me of my question. "Mom, if God doesn't always do miracles to answer our prayers, what does He do? Does He just not answer them?"

"Sometimes it seems that way," she answered. "Like when Nina died. If only a miracle can fix what's wrong, then I guess His answer is No. But I think God uses people to answer prayers."

"How?"

"Christians are supposed to be God's hands in this world. We're supposed to do His work. If a family is hungry and has no food, God can answer their prayer for help by sending a Christian to help. That's why our church has a program to help people in need."

I was still confused. "But how do Christians know who needs help? How does the prayer to God get to them?"

She smiled. "That's another kind of miracle,

DETECTIVE ZACK

Zack. If your mind is open to God, He uses the Holy Spirit to make you aware of a need."

I thought about that. "He sends you a clue?"

"That's right," she said with a laugh. "And if you're paying attention, He can help you figure it out and know what to do to help. Also, sometimes I think we have to help answer our own prayers."

Now I was really confused. "Answer our own prayers?"

"Think about it," she said. "Did you ever pray for help when you were taking a test at school?"

"Sure," I answered. "I want a good grade."

"Well, what else did you do besides pray?"

I thought for a second. "I studied and did my homework. Oh, I see what you're saying. I helped answer my prayer by being ready to take the test."

"Right." Then she laughed. "Your trap reminds of something I never told your Uncle Travis. One summer, he decided to catch wild animals and sell them—you know, rabbits and squirrels and things. He was trying to make money, but I didn't think it was right to catch those poor little animals. Anyway, he built some wooden traps and put them in the woods. I got very upset and stomped to my room. First, I knelt by my bed and prayed that no animals would be caught in the traps. Then later, when he was in school, I went out and kicked them all to pieces!"

"Mom!" I had to laugh. "I guess you really did answer your own prayer."

"Hey," Uncle Travis called up the stairs, "you guys need to come down and see this."

This time, the TV screen was covered by a big blue sign. It said "Hurricane Watch."

Prayer Clues

Sometimes, God uses people to answer prayers. Christians are supposed to be God's hands in this world and do the things He needs to have done.

God tells Christians what needs to be done by using the Holy Spirit to send them a clue. If they're paying attention, God can help them figure it out and know what to do to help.

Sometimes we have to help answer our own prayers.

CHAPTER TEN

The Mystery Is Solved—Wrong!

*Hurricane Jacque
Winds—110 m.p.h.*

"We are now under a hurricane watch," a voice announced. "This means that hurricane-force winds are possible in the watch area in the next forty-eight hours. Hurricane Jacque has slowed down and is getting stronger every hour. With winds already over one hundred miles per hour, this is a dangerous storm. Please stay tuned to your local news and weather for up-to-the-minute coverage of this situation."

"We'd better make a run to town," Grandpa said. "There are a few things we might need if we lose power."

Kayla looked worried. "You don't think the storm is coming here, do you, Grandpa? Sonia says they always turn away at the last minute."

He shrugged. "Better safe than sorry, I always say. Now, what do we need?"

Dusty and I ended up going to town with Grandpa in his pickup truck. "Wow, it's really crowded," Dusty said as we pulled into the grocery-store parking lot.

"Everyone's thinking the same thing we are," Grandpa said. "Now, where's our list?"

"I'll get the batteries we need," I said. I wanted to be sure to get new ones for my flashlight. Dusty ran to get candles. Grandpa loaded up on a lot of food in cans and boxes.

We were almost to the checkout stand when we nearly ran into someone. "Oh, hi, Sonia," I said. She was there with her dad. "Looks like you guys are here for the same reason we are."

Mr. Tillman took one look at our basket and sniffed. "Certainly not. That storm's not even headed our way. We're just picking up a few groceries."

"Hey, Sonia," Dusty said, "we caught a black-and-white rabbit in the woods this morning. It's not yours, is it?"

Sonia's mouth fell open. But before she could say anything, her dad did. "Sonia, that better not be your rabbit. I told you I didn't want any rabbits around."

The Mystery Is Solved—Wrong!

"I did what you told me," she said. "It's not mine." She looked like she had a hundred questions, but Mr. Tillman dragged her away.

"Next stop, the hardware store," Grandpa said when we had all the groceries in the truck. The hardware store was even more crowded. "Looks like everyone needs hurricane-prevention supplies."

"Grandpa, you can't prevent a hurricane," I protested.

He laughed. "I know, but you can prevent some of the damage." He picked out several rolls of tape and some plywood while he explained. "We'll put the plywood over the big windows in the living room to protect them from flying objects if the wind picks up. The other windows are smaller and not so expensive. We'll just tape across the glass in big crisscross patterns. That way, if the window breaks, the glass won't shatter all over the place."

"This is going to be fun!" Dusty decided.

Grandpa rubbed his chin. "Hhm, we're going to need something to take the plywood back off, and I lost my good crowbar last week."

I just happened to be staring at a short little crowbar when he said it. "Grandpa, here's one. How about it?"

"Well, it's not very big, but I guess it'll do. Come on, let's go."

Dusty and I taped windows while Grandpa and Uncle Trav nailed up the plywood. "This is fun," Dusty said. "It's like getting ready for a war. We've preparing for an enemy invasion!"

I picked up the little crowbar. "Well, we've got weapons to fight back!"

When we finished, Dusty and I stacked the leftover tape and the rest of the tools in the barn. Even with the wind whistling outside, I heard something in the feed room. "Come on," I whispered. "Maybe this time, we can catch whoever's taking the feed."

We caught them, all right. It was only Kayla and the rabbit. "Hi, guys. I think he's starting to like me."

Dusty told her about meeting Sonia at the store. "She sure was surprised to hear about this rabbit. It's definitely not hers. I guess we'll never know where it came from."

"I guess we'll never figure out what's going on around here either," I said with a sigh. "I hate to leave a mystery unsolved."

"Let's go look at the Miller barn one more time," Kayla suggested. "Maybe we can figure it out." On the way there, she repeated the things we did know. "Either those escaped prisoners were hiding out in Millers' barn, or Mr. Tillman was trying to hurt Grandma's chickens by turning Lucifer loose and stealing chicken feed."

"If it's the prisoners, then why is chicken feed missing?" Dusty asked.

Kayla shrugged. "Maybe they got really, really hungry?"

"If it's Mr. Tillman, why would he break into Millers' barn?"

Kayla raised her hands. "Maybe that's where he's feeding Lucifer?" She stomped her foot. "I don't know! You figure it out."

When we reached the front of the barn, I looked through the crack between the big doors again. "I think there are more footprints than before," I said. "But I still don't know how someone is getting in."

I walked over to the big tree and sat down. And there, right between my feet, was a nice shoeprint. "Hey, look. A shoeprint, with a big circle in the heel, just like the one we found in Grandpa's feed room."

We looked around, but there weren't any others near the barn. "How can there just be one print? I know the ground is grassy out past the tree, but it's all dirt between the tree and the barn."

Then, over the noise of the wind, I heard a *thump* sound. I listened until I heard it again. "Listen," I said to the others. Following the sound, I looked up. When the wind gusted, the big loft doors up above moved out a few inches, then back in—*thump*.

"That's it," I said. "When we talked about this barn being just like Grandpa's, I should have thought of the loft doors."

"You're right," Kayla agreed. "Look, that tree limb leads right up to the doors. And the doors open just enough for someone to stick their hand in and unlatch them. Then all they'd have to do is step inside."

I walked over to the crack again and looked in. "You can see that the footprints inside lead to and from the ladder to the loft. Well, it really was the escaped prisoners, then. They were hiding in Grandpa's barn. That's why we saw the shoeprint there. Then they came up here and climbed the tree into this barn." I shook my head. "They probably climbed down and left days ago."

"Do you want to go inside and find out for sure?" Dusty asked. Before I had time to answer, we heard Mom shouting from the farm.

"Must be suppertime," I said. "Let's come back after we eat."

The Mystery Is Solved—Wrong!

As we sat down to eat, a few big drops of rain spattered against the windows. "That wind seems to be getting stronger," Grandma said. "We could be in for a rough night."

I decided to go ahead and tell. "Uh, Grandpa, I think I know where those escaped prisoners were a few days ago."

"Oh, been listening to the news, have you? Well, it was a relief to me to find out that they turned themselves in over in the next county. They never were anywhere near here."

I just stared at him for a second. "Zack, chew with your mouth closed," Mom said. Kayla's mouth was hanging open too. Dusty leaned over to whisper.

"If it wasn't them, who was it?"

I had no idea.

Suddenly, the sound from the TV stopped. Everyone turned at the same time to stare at the screen. The picture had been replaced by one of those blue screens. "Uh-oh," Dusty whispered.

Then a voice spoke. "This is the Emergency Broadcast System. A hurricane warning has been issued for this area. Please stand by for information on this developing emergency. A hurricane warning has been issued for this area."

"Oh, my," Mom said softly.

DETECTIVE ZACK

Then the meteorologist came on. "Hurricane Jacque has double-crossed us. With one-hundred-and-ten-mile-per-hour winds, Jacque has turned and is headed straight toward us."

Prayer Clues

The Bible says, Ask, and it will be given to you. What if you don't get what you ask for? Is the Bible wrong?

Mystery in the Barn

We found another shoeprint like the one in the feed room by the tree in front of Millers' barn. Then we noticed the loft doors could be opened by someone who climbed out on a limb. So we decided that it must have really been the escaped prisoners and that they probably left days ago.

We were wrong. The prisoners already turned themselves in. Then who's stealing the chicken feed and going in the barn?

Words to Remember

Hurricane watch: A weather warning that means that hurricane-force winds (over seventy-four miles per hour) are possible within the next forty-eight hours.

Hurricane warning: Big Trouble!

CHAPTER ELEVEN

Hurricane Warning

Hurricane Jacque
Winds—110 m.p.h.

No one in the house said a word.

"As you heard, a hurricane warning has been issued. That means that hurricane-force winds are expected in this area within the next twelve hours. But because of this sudden turn, I expect our winds to be gusting over eighty miles per hour before midnight. If you have not already taken steps to protect your property, finish that up quickly, and get to a shelter."

Grandma spoke first. "Well, Grandpa," she said, "it looks like you did the right thing this afternoon. The Lord has His eye on us. All we have to do is hunker down and wait out the storm here where it's safe."

DETECTIVE ZACK

Grandpa started to say something, but he was interrupted.

Bang! Bang! Bang! Someone was pounding on the front door. "Who would be out at a time like this?" Mom wondered. When Grandpa opened the door, there stood Mr. Tillman. His hair was standing up all over, and his eyes looked almost as wild.

"Sonia's gone!" he blurted out.

Grandpa pulled him inside. "What happened?"

"We had an argument on the way home from the store. She said I didn't love her and that I didn't want her around. I snapped back the way I do too many times. She ran to her room as soon as we got home. When I went to tell her how sorry I am, she was gone!"

"I'm sure she didn't go far," Grandma started to say. But he interrupted.

"I know I'm too gruff sometimes, but I do love her! I was driving around, looking for her, when I heard about the hurricane. You've got to help me find her!"

"Of course we will," Grandpa said. "We still have nearly an hour before dark. We'll drive around and look for her. She can't have gone far. Come on."

Mom grabbed her car keys too. "Zack, can I borrow your flashlight? You and Kayla stay here and help Grandma. We'll be back soon." Uncle Trav followed her out.

Grandma sat back down in front of the TV. Before she said a word to any of us, she started praying. "Oh, Lord, watch over Sonia. Wherever she is, keep her safe until they find her. Guide their minds to where she is. Keep us all safe in this storm. In Jesus' name. Amen."

"Amen," Kayla echoed quietly. We listened to the wind howl with one ear and the news announcer with the other for a few minutes; then Dusty saw something outside.

"Grandma, isn't that one of your chickens flying across the yard?" We all rushed to the window and tried to see between the strips of tape.

"Oh no," Grandma said. "It looks like the chicken-coop door is banging in the wind. I was going to make sure that was locked up after supper. It's scaring all the chickens out into the wind."

"Come on, Grandma. Let's get 'em," I said. As we rushed out into the yard, I was amazed at the wind. "Wow, this is almost hard to walk against," I shouted to Dusty.

"Just wait until the hurricane gets here," he shouted back.

Grandma led us right to the chicken pen. Just as we got the gate open, another chicken flapped her wings and got caught in the wind. "Let her go," Grandma shouted. "Let's get the others back inside the coop."

But before we could get to it, the coop door snapped around again with a gust of wind and broke. As it fell to the ground, two more chickens came dashing out. "Now what are we going to do?" Kayla shouted.

Grandma grabbed both chickens before they could sail away. "We'll have to put them in the barn," she said. "Come open the door. We'll put them in the feed room."

But before she could get back, another hen escaped. The wind blew it right past the barn. "This isn't going to work," I shouted to Grandma when she got back. "There are too many chickens to carry in one or two at a time."

"What else can we do?"

For some reason, I thought of what Grandpa did when there were a lot of feed sacks to unload. "The feed chute," I said. "We can push them down the feed chute."

"But it's nailed closed. We'd have to find a crowbar."

"Zack," Dusty said, "where's that new one?"

For a second, I was almost too shocked to speak. "It's right here!" I finally said, reaching into my jacket pocket. "I never put it away."

"Go!" Grandma commanded. She grabbed two more chickens and handed them to Kayla. Dusty and I ran to the barn. With me prying and him pulling, we had the board off in no time.

Grandma was waiting. She stuffed one chicken, then the other, down the chute. *Bock-bock-bock!* Kayla's went next.

"It's working!" I shouted. Grandma gave me a smile, then stuffed in another chicken. As I pushed one in, a swirl of wind brought a strange kind of smell up from the feed room. I thought for a second. *Where have I smelled that before?*

I shook it off and went back for another hen. When Grandma shoved Old Red Top in, we were finished. We all raced around to the barn door. "It feels great to be out of that wind for a minute," I said. "Grandma, do you want us to go after the ones that blew away?"

"No, we'll look for them tomorrow," she said as she tried to smooth her hair down. It didn't help much. "Let's get these settled and head back to the house."

I followed her into the feed room, and in spite of all the clucking and commotion, the smell hit me again. This time, I figured out what it was. "Hey, your chickens are scaring the rabbit," I said.

Grandma reached into an open bag and pulled out a handful of feed. When that hit the floor, the clucking quieted down. "They'll be fine for tonight. We'll worry about the mess they'll make tomorrow. Let's go."

Dusty and Kayla were staring out at the yard. Leaves and small branches almost covered the ground. "It's getting dark fast," Kayla said. "And the wind's getting stronger. I hope Sonia's OK."

Grandma gave her a hug. "We prayed that God would keep her safe, right? That's all we can do for now. I'm sure she's somewhere just as safe and warm as this barn. Come on. I'll race you to the house!"

They ran through the falling leaves, but it took Dusty and me both to pull the barn door shut. Somehow, Grandma's words were still bouncing through my brain. Then they stuck.

"Dusty!" I grabbed him and pushed the barn door back open. "Come here and smell this."

"What? Are you crazy? Smell what?"

"The rabbit cage." I wanted him to tell me I wasn't crazy. "Where have you smelled that before?"

He bent down and took a sniff. "Whew! That's a strong smell. And not a nice one."

"That's exactly what you said before. The light,

the chicken feed, the footprints, the rabbit! That's it! Come on!" I turned and ran back out to the barn door.

Dusty raced after me. "Zack! What is it? Come on where?"

We stepped out and pulled the door closed behind us. "Do you have your flashlight?" I asked. He nodded. "Then let's go."

He grabbed my arm. "Let's go where?"

"I know where Sonia is," I said. "And we have to go get her—before the hurricane gets here."

Mystery in the Barn

The light, the chicken feed, the footprint, the rabbit! I've got it!

Words to Remember

Hurricane warning: Hurricane-force winds are expected in this area within the next twelve hours. Find a safe place to hide, or get out fast!

CHAPTER TWELVE

Trapped Like Rabbits

Hurricane Jacque Winds—110 m.p.h.

"You know where Sonia is because the rabbit stinks?" Dusty shouted. "Where?"

I huddled down next to the barn wall and explained. "You smelled that same smell at the Miller barn, through the feed chute, remember?"

"That's right," he agreed, nodding his head. "So there's rabbits inside. So what?"

"Remember, Sonia's dad wouldn't let her keep her rabbit. But she couldn't just let it go, and she didn't want to give it away. So she kept it—in Millers' barn."

Dusty started nodding. "She'd have no problem climbing that tree to get in the loft doors."

"And that's why the chicken feed is missing. She

needed to feed it something, since she couldn't let it go outside to eat. Anyway, her fight with her dad was probably about the rabbit that he wouldn't let her keep. She thinks he doesn't love her."

Dusty finished it up. "So if she ran away because of her rabbit, that's where she went. No one would ever find her in Millers' barn. And she doesn't know the hurricane is coming here! Come on, let's go!"

"Zack!" Kayla's voice was hard to hear over the wind. "Zack, come on! Come back to the house!" She and Grandma were in the doorway, motioning us to join them.

I cupped my hands around my mouth. "We know where Sonia is! We're going to get her!"

I could see them discussing what they heard. Finally, she shouted back. "Wait, we'll come with you!"

"No! You have to stay there and wait for Grandpa! We'll hurry!" I grabbed Dusty's jacket sleeve, and we turned toward the Miller barn. As soon as we stepped out away from Grandpa's barn, the wind was blowing straight at us. Millers' barn seemed a long way away.

"I can't even stand up straight," Dusty yelled in my ear.

"Hang on to my jacket," I answered. "Let's duck

down as low as we can." Leaning over so far we would have fallen over any other day, we slowly stepped up the path.

"It may be hard to climb the tree in this wind," I shouted over my shoulder as we reached the side of the barn and stopped to rest.

"It's going to be harder than you think," he said, pointing ahead. Then I saw it. Most of the tree was lying on the ground!

We raced as far as we could go along the barn wall without stepping into the wind again. "It cracked and broke off," I said. "All that's left up in the air is a stub."

"So how do we get in?" he asked.

I shrugged. "Let's find out if she's really here." We walked back to the front door and started pounding. "Sonia! Are you in there, Sonia?" Dusty took a turn shouting; then we listened. Nothing.

"It doesn't prove anything," I said. "She probably can't hear us. I can barely hear us myself!"

"So what do we do?" Dusty asked again.

"There's only one other way in," I reminded him. "The feed chute."

"Oh no," he answered. "I'm not going down that slide into the dark. Who knows what's down there after all these years."

"We know what's down there," I said. "It's a

rabbit. And probably a girl. Come on!" We walked around the edge and crawled slowly into the wind toward the chute. But when we got to it, I wasn't so sure either. "It does look dark—and dangerous."

Dusty nodded—then winced. "Ow!" he said, putting his hand on his neck. "What was that? It stung like a bee!"

Then one hit my forehead. "Yow! What is it?" I put my hand up to stop the blood I felt trickling down. But when I looked at my hand, it was water. "Hey, it's rain. Raindrops being blown by the wind!" Suddenly, it started raining faster. And it wasn't coming down, it was coming sideways. "It feels like bullets, even through my clothes. Even going down the chute would be better than this!"

"OK," Dusty said, reaching for his flashlight and handing it to me. "But you go first!"

Sticking my head into the chute wasn't easy. It was just too small and too dark. But a few more rain pellets in the rear sent me sliding forward and down. "Whoa!" I shouted. I tried to hold the flashlight out in front. Then I gave up and just covered my head. All of a sudden, I hit bottom and tasted dust.

Even in the dark, I knew it was the same smell, only stronger. I clicked on the light just in time to be hit in the back of the head.

It was Dusty. "Hey. Hey!" he shouted. "Where are you?"

"You're sitting on me," I finally managed to say. I flicked the light in his eyes. "Get off." When I rolled over to sit up, the light shone across the floor. Everywhere it touched, I saw the reflection of eyes.

"Zack, do you see what I see?" Dusty asked. "Kayla was right—this room is full of rats!"

We both stood up quickly, and I saw eyes reflecting from all over. "It's—it's . . ." I looked a little closer. "It's rabbits!" I walked closer to the nearest ones. "They're all rabbits—black-and-white ones."

Dusty was amazed. "There must be twenty or thirty in this room. No wonder we could smell them. But where's . . ."

The door to the room was opening slowly. "Who's there?" Dusty shouted.

Sonia's face appeared in the doorway. "Zack? Dusty? Is it really you?" I could see shiny trails of tears down her dusty face.

"Well, yeah, it's us," I said. "Did you know . . ."

She interrupted. "You came to get me. I prayed, and you came."

"We knew you were gone," Dusty said. "And Zack figured out that you had to be here."

Sonia smiled and sniffed, then frowned. "How did you know I was gone?"

"Your dad," I told her. "He came and begged us to come and help find you. He was worried sick!"

That seemed amazing to her. "Really?"

"He probably still is. The hurricane is coming, you know," Dusty said.

She nodded. "That's what I thought. I heard the wind get louder, but I didn't want to leave. Then the tree blew over, and I couldn't get out." Then her face clouded over. "Now you guys can't get out either. We're all trapped in here."

"What do you mean, we can't get out?" Dusty asked, marching over to the door. "Let's get out there and try."

"I've been trying," Sonia claimed as we hurried out into the main barn. "The doors are all bolted and locked. The windows all have bars. The only way in and out was the loft doors. And now that won't work unless you want to fall twenty or thirty feet."

"What about the chute?" I asked.

Dusty sat down in the dim light from the windows. "I don't think so," he said. "It fell apart when I slid down. Wait a minute, Zack. Grandma knew we were going to find Sonia. She'll tell them to come get us."

I had already thought of that. "I don't think so. I forgot to tell them where we were going."

Dusty almost argued; then he gave up. "I guess all we can do is sit and wait."

"And one more thing," I added. "We can pray."

"That's right," Sonia agreed. "It worked before. I prayed, and you guys came. And believe me, this is better than being here alone. In the dark. In a hurricane."

I walked to the window and closed my eyes. "God, we need some help. Please send someone to rescue us. Or keep us safe here. Thank You. In Jesus' name. Amen."

"Amen," Sonia echoed.

When I opened my eyes, I could see that the rain had stopped. The wind was whipping the trees around like crazy, but I could see all the way to the house. *Kayla and Grandma must be right there by the door, wondering where we are.* The porch seemed to blink because of all the branches between here and there whipping all around.

Wait a minute, I thought. *If I can see that light . . .* "That's it! Dusty, give me your flashlight."

"You've already got it," he said.

"Oh yeah." I pulled it out and clicked on the light. Pointing it out the window, I clicked it on and off, on and off. While I was watching, all the lights in the house went out.

"Hey, don't waste the batteries. That's the only light we'll have all night." He watched for a minute. "What are you doing?"

"Helping God answer my prayer," I told him. I kept the light going for about five minutes, then turned it off. Suddenly, it seemed very dark.

The roaring of the wind got even louder. From the snapping and crashing sounds outside, I knew trees were falling and limbs were breaking. *Maybe we should just be thankful to be inside somewhere.*

As the roaring got louder, the big doors at the end began to move. I clicked on the light. "Look," Sonia said. "The doors are bending in. The wind is going to blow them open! Get back!"

We backed all the way against the opposite wall. Then the wood holding the bolt started snapping like rifle shots.

Then with a mighty bang, the doors exploded in!

CHAPTER THIRTEEN

Rescue From the Hurricane

Hurricane Jacque
Winds—110 m.p.h.

Sonia screamed. Dusty threw up his hands. I ducked my face into my jacket. Pieces of the door flew all the way back to where we were standing. The wind rushed in, and with it came light.

Headlights, to be exact. Attached to Grandpa's truck. The doors popped open. "Sonia? Are you OK, baby?"

"Daddy?" Sonia met her dad halfway across the floor and buried herself in his arms.

"Zack? Dusty? Are you OK?" Grandpa wasn't far behind.

"We're fine, Grandpa. And glad to see you!"

I think he carried us back to the truck. "Let's get out of here," he called to Mr. Tillman. We all squished into the cab, but no one minded being crowded. Not at all.

"It's getting bad out here," Grandpa said as he steered toward the Tillmans'. "We had to go around this way because that tree is down." He pulled right up onto the Tillmans' carport. "Are you sure you'll be all right?" he asked. "You're welcome to get your wife and join us."

"We'll be fine," Mr. Tillman said, looking at Sonia. "Everything's fine now. Thanks for everything. Especially you, boys. I never would have found her without you. Thank God you knew where to look."

"That's right, Daddy," Sonia said. "You should thank God. I prayed, and He sent Zack and Dusty."

As we backed away, it was raining so hard it was almost impossible to see through the windshield. "Well, we'll just go slow," Grandpa said. "And if we run into something, we'll just back up and try again."

After driving over two trees and around another one, we finally made it back to the farm. Mom and Uncle Trav raced outside as soon as the truck stopped right by the front door. "Come on," Uncle Trav said, scooping us both up. In just a few seconds, the winds and rain were shut outside.

A few minutes later, the hugging and crying and laughing slowed down. Grandma wrapped us in blankets while Kayla brought us all some hot chocolate. "It's the last of the hot water. Enjoy it."

"Come on," Grandpa said. "Everyone to the basement. This storm isn't over yet."

"I saw your light up in Millers' barn," Kayla said when we got settled down there. "Everyone had just returned, and Mom almost blew her top when she found out you were gone. I told them where to find you. Sonia was the one who was in the barn that night you saw the light, wasn't she?"

"How did you know she was there tonight?" Mom asked.

I smiled. "Grandma's prayer worked." Everyone looked surprised. "Grandma prayed that Sonia would be safe, and God started answering the prayer. Actually, He was working on it all day."

"Explain this to me," Grandpa said.

"You remember that crowbar?" I asked him. "It was right there in the store when you wanted to buy one. But it was small enough that I still had it in my pocket when we needed it for the chickens."

Grandma explained about the chickens. "Thanks to these guys and to Zack's quick thinking, we saved most of them."

"Thanks to having that crowbar in my pocket," I added. "And that's not all. When I was standing there by the feed chute, I smelled something that I had smelled before. When we went in and I saw the rabbit, I knew that's what it was."

"Wait a minute." Kayla snapped her fingers. "That's what we smelled in the chute at Millers' barn. Was there a rabbit in there?"

"A rabbit?" Dusty laughed. "There were dozens of rabbits in that room, all with black-and-white spots. They were everywhere!"

"That's right," I said. "And that's what started me thinking. Then when we were leaving the barn, Grandma told you that because she had prayed, she was sure that Sonia was someplace safe. Someplace safe like the barn."

Grandma nodded.

"When I heard that, all the pieces clicked. Someone was climbing the tree to get into Millers' barn through the loft. Sonia could do that. It was her shoeprint we were seeing—the one with the circle in the heel. Someone was stealing chicken feed. Sonia needed it because she had to hide the rabbit from her father. And being kept inside meant she had to feed it."

"And many other rabbits, it seems," Grandma added.

"Sonia's fight with her dad was probably about the rabbit she couldn't keep, since we told her about our rabbit in the store. So she ran away to where her rabbit was. When Dusty and I slid into her rabbit room, she was sure that we were the answer to her prayer."

Kayla was surprised. "Prayer? She told us she didn't believe in prayer."

"I guess maybe she does now. Anyway, Grandpa, I think God was guiding my mind, giving me clues even before I needed them. I think He led us to the crowbar. I think He was answering Grandma's prayer even before she prayed it."

Dusty spoke up. "Zack prayed, too, when we were trapped in Millers' barn. And then he had the idea of flashing the light at you."

"Just helping answer my own prayer, Mom," I said. She smiled and shook her head.

Crack! Crash!

The loud noise from upstairs quieted everyone for a moment. The roar of the wind was so loud that we couldn't even hear the thunder. Grandpa got up. "I have about a hundred questions, Zack, but I'd better go check on that."

Dusty was telling them about the bullet rain when it happened again.

Crack! Crash! Smash!

This time, the whole house shook.

"Grandpa?" Kayla called. Uncle Trav was already headed up the stairs.

"I'm OK," Grandpa called down. "But I think we should all stay in the basement until the storm is over." He pushed Uncle Trav ahead of him back down the stairs and shut the door behind them. Then he took a seat on the couch. Finally, he seemed to notice that everyone was staring at him. "What?"

"What happened upstairs? What crashed? What's broken?" Everyone shouted their question at the same time.

"Well, the good news is, the living-room windows aren't broken yet." Then he turned to Mom. "The bad news is, there's a tree in your bedroom."

Prayer Clues

God was answering Grandma's prayers before she prayed them. Was He giving me clues so I could answer Sonia's prayer? I'm sure He was helping me. He helped me think of how to answer my own prayer too!

Mystery in the Barn

Sonia was the person in the Miller barn. She was taking the chicken feed for her rabbit. It was locked inside the barn because she was hiding it from her father. It was her footprints in the feed room and under the tree.

CHAPTER FOURTEEN

Secret in the Storm

Now that we're heading home again, I think I was right in the first place—being in a hurricane is amazing! I'm not sure I'd ever want to do it again, but I have a lot to tell Dad and Alex about.

The newspeople say that Hurricane Jacque was one of the most expensive disasters of the year. I know it's going to take a long time to recover from it. At least, at Grandpa's house it is.

The night of the storm, a lot of things were broken. The chicken coop blew away again. But this time, the chickens weren't in it. Some of Grandma's windows were broken. But the worst thing was the tree that fell on their house.

It was the tree right outside of Aunt Nina's

room. Actually, just one big limb came in through the window. But it destroyed the window, broke the bed, and messed up almost everything else in the room. And then lots of rain came in.

After Grandpa sawed off the limbs sticking in the house, Mr. Tillman dragged the trunk away with his tractor. I helped Mom clean up the room.

"This is really awful," Mom said as she dumped another load of wet blankets into a basket. "But I'm very, very happy no one was in here to get hurt." She turned and pushed my hair back. "You really scared me by being out in that hurricane, you know."

"I know. I scared me too. But I guess it turned out OK. What do you want to do with the desk?" Aunt Nina's desk was lying on the floor with a broken leg.

"I guess we'll just lean it against the wall for now," she answered. "Maybe Grandpa can fix it." When we lifted it back up and set it aside, I saw something white on the floor.

"Here's more trash, Mom," I said, tossing the old envelope to her. She almost tossed it into the bag, but stopped.

"Zack, it's a letter," she said, with a strange look on her face. "It's a letter to you."

The first thing I saw when she handed it to me

was the return address in the corner. "It's from Aunt Nina. Why didn't she mail it to me?"

"It must have fallen behind her desk or something. It must have been one of the last letters she wrote."

I tore open the envelope as carefully as I could and unfolded the letter.

"Dear Zack," it said.

"How is my favorite nephew? I hope things are going all right for you in school. I guess things could be better here, but I'm still smiling.

"Zack, I want you to know how sad I am that I won't get to see you grow up. But I'm looking forward to seeing how you turned out when we get to heaven! I thank God every day for the wonderful life He gave me and for the wonderful family I had for all these years.

"Don't be mad at God, Zack. In this sinful world, people are going to get sick and die. If He wants to heal me, I know He can. But if that's not for the best, I trust Him. He knows best, and I know He loves me more than you and I can even imagine.

"Don't miss me too much. Just remember the happy times we had together—and start planning for more happy times in heaven.

"Love forever, Aunt Nina."

I guess Mom and I both cried a little after that.

But it was a happy cry. I guess if Aunt Nina could trust God to do what's best, so can I.

We never found the chickens that were blown away by the wind. Sonia came over while we were helping Grandma put the chicken-pen fence back up. "I'm sorry I stole your chicken feed," she told Grandma. "I'll work to pay you back." Grandma just hugged her.

Dusty couldn't wait to ask a question. "Where did all those rabbits come from?"

Sonia shook her head. "That's why Daddy didn't want me to keep Oreo. She was expecting babies. He said we'd have rabbits all over the place before long. I guess he was right. That's why I kept having to take more chicken feed. I had twenty-two rabbits in there!"

"What about the one we caught in the woods?" I asked.

"He must have escaped through the slot after you guys pulled the board off. I didn't even know he was gone."

Kayla patted her friend's hand. "Well, he's right here in the barn when you want him. What are you going to do with all those rabbits?"

"Daddy's going to help me give them away. And he said I could keep Oreo—but we're having her fixed right away. No more baby bunnies!"

"OK," Grandma finally said, "let's get those chickens out of that barn. They'll have to be happy with this old doghouse until we can rebuild the chicken coop."

We shuttled them out, one by one, and dropped them in their pen. They were so happy to be outside pecking at the dirt they almost forgot to cluck. But not Old Red Top!

Err-erer—eroo!

Then we heard an answer. *Err-erer-aack!*

"It's Lucifer!" Dusty shouted. "But where is he?" By following the scratching sounds, we found him in the pile of boards that used to be the chicken coop. "Grandma, he's trapped inside!"

"How about that," she said. "Lucifer was even tougher than the hurricane."

We had to get Uncle Trav to get him out, but once he was free, Lucifer was as mean as ever. Uncle Trav wore big leather gloves and carried the rooster over to an empty box. "You'll wait right there for a free trip home."

I thought being in a hurricane would be exciting. I was right about that! It was almost too exciting. But we solved the mystery of the light in Millers' barn and the missing chicken feed. And we helped Sonia fix her problem with her rabbit and her problem with her dad.

DETECTIVE ZACK

I guess I learned that the Bible is right again. God really does answer prayers—if you pay attention to the clues. I'm glad I learned that God is someone I can talk to—someone who listens and cares.

I figured out the real secret in the storm—God was with me, even in the middle of a hurricane. Whatever mystery there is about God, this part is no secret. You can trust God—no matter what happens.